Curious George
Home Run
Jorge el curioso™
El jonrón

📖 bookspring

I will read my book again and again!
¡Voy a leer mi libro una y otra vez!

This book belongs to/Este libro le pertenece a:

_____

Write your name on the line and keep this book for your very own.
Escribe tu nombre en la línea y guarda tu libro para siempre.

Adaptation by Erica Zappy
Based on the TV series teleplay written by Lazar Sario
Translated by Carlos E. Calvo
Adaptado por Erica Zappy
Basado en el guión para televisión escrito por Lazar Sario
Traducido por Carlos E. Calvo

Houghton Mifflin Harcourt Publishing Company
Boston New York 2012

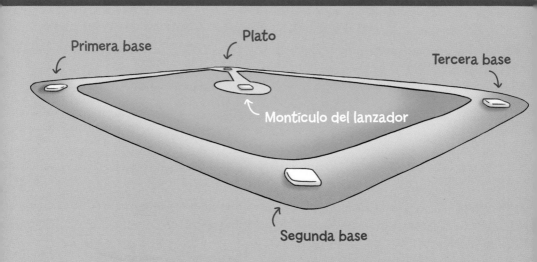

Primera base

Plato

Tercera base

Montículo del lanzador

Segunda base

For information about permission to reproduce selections from this book, write to Permissions, Houghton Mifflin Harcourt Publishing Company, 215 Park Avenue South, New York, New York 10003.

Library of Congress Cataloging-in-Publication is on file.

ISBN: 978-0-547-69117-6 paper-over-board
ISBN: 978-0-547-69118-3 paperback
ISBN: 978-0-547-69122-0 paper-over-board bilingual
ISBN: 978-0-547-69114-5 paperback bilingual

Design by Anjali Pala

www.hmhbooks.com

Manufactured in Singapore
TWP 10 9 8 7 6 5 4 3 2 1
4500332286

AGE	GRADES	GUIDED READING LEVEL	READING RECOVERY LEVEL	LEXILE ® LEVEL	SPANISH LEXII
5-7	1-2	I	15-16	460L	470L

Today George was going to his first baseball game.
His friend Marco was playing.

Hoy Jorge fue a su primer partido de béisbol.
Su amigo Marco jugaba en el partido.

Marco's team was the Cubby Bears.
They were playing the Tiger Babies.
Marco wanted to hit a home run.
He practiced batting.

El equipo de Marco son los Oseznos.
Jugaban contra los Tigrecitos.
Marco deseaba hacer un jonrón.
Practicaba con el bate.

Uh-oh.

The scorekeeper was sick.

"Will you help, George?" asked the coach.

Of course! George is always happy to help.

¡Oh, oh!
El tanteador estaba enfermo.
—¿Jorge, nos podrías ayudar? —le preguntó el entrenador.
¡Por supuesto! A Jorge siempre le gusta ayudar.

"Every time a team scores, you hang a new number," said Marco. That seemed easy!
But there were lots of numbers.

—Cada vez que un equipo anote un punto, pones un nuevo número —dijo Marco. ¡Parecía fácil!
Pero había un montón de números.

George waited and waited.
Sometimes baseball moves very slowly!
By the third inning, there were still no numbers to hang.

**Jorge esperaba y esperaba.
¡A veces el béisbol va muy despacio!
Ya era la tercera entrada y aún no había puesto ningún número.**

Finally, there was some action!
Marco got a hit. His teammate got one too!
Marco slid into home plate and scored one run.

¡Por fin empezó la acción!
Marco bateó y llegó a la primera base. ¡Su compañero también!
Marco resbaló hasta el plato y anotó una carrera.

Now George could put a number on the scoreboard. He pulled the number 5 out of the box and put it up.

Ahora Jorge podía poner un número en el marcador. Sacó el número 5 de la caja y lo puso.

"That's the wrong number!" said Marco.
George pulled another number from the box. He put up
the number 8.

—¡Ese número está mal! —dijo Marco.
Jorge sacó otro número de la caja. Puso el número 8.

"Use a lower number! You need to put the numbers up in order," said Marco.
Order? What did that mean? George was curious.

—¡Pon un número más bajo! Debes poner los números en orden —le dijo Marco.
¿En orden? ¿Qué significa eso? Jorge sintió curiosidad.

Marco showed George how to put the numbers in order.
"Like this: 1, 2, 3, 4, 5, 6, 7, 8, 9, and 10.
Now you try," said Marco.

**Marco le mostró a Jorge cómo poner los números en orden.
—Así: 1, 2, 3, 4, 5, 6, 7, 8, 9 y 10.
Ahora prueba tú —le explicó Marco.**

George practiced putting the numbers in order.
It worked! He kept score until the game was tied at 4–4.

**Jorge practicó cómo poner los números en orden.
¡Funcionó! Contó los puntos hasta que el partido empató 4 a 4.**

George heard a lot of noise coming from the snack counter. He could help hand out snacks.

Jorge escuchó mucho ruido que venía del quiosco. Quizás podría ayudar a servir refrigerios.

George handed out the food order for number 17.
Then 14.

"Wait," a customer said.

"The number 14 comes before 17."

"Yeah! And 12 comes before 13!" exclaimed another.

Jorge sirvió el pedido número 17.
Después el 14.
—¡Un momento! —dijó un cliente—. El número 14 está
antes que el 17.
—¡Sí! ¡Y el 12 viene antes que el 13! —exclamó otro.

George was confused.
"Do you know your numbers?" the girl at the snack bar aske
He counted on his fingers from 1 to 10.

Jorge estaba confundido.
—¿No sabes los números? —le preguntó la chica del quiosco.
Jorge contó del 1 al 10.

"Here's how to find out what comes after 10," she said. She held her hand over the 1 in the number 11 and the 1 in the number 12.

—Así puedes saber qué viene después de 10 —le dijo la chica. Y cubrió el primer 1 del número 11 con la mano, y también el 1 del número 12.

Now George knew that 11 comes before 12, just like
1 comes before 2.
He gave the customers their snacks in order.

**Ahora Jorge sabía que el 11 viene antes que el 12, igual que
el 1 viene antes que el 2.
Y les dio a los clientes sus refrigerios en orden.**

When George returned to the game, Marco was at bat.
But he had hurt his foot.
George would run the bases for Marco!

**Cuando Jorge volvió al partido, Marco estaba bateando.
Pero se había lastimado el pie.
¡Jorge llegaría a las bases por Marco!**

If Marco got three strikes,
he would get an out.
Strike one! Strike two!

**Si Marco lograba tres strikes
conseguiría un *out*.
¡Primer *strike*! ¡Segundo *strike*!**

Crack! Marco
hit the ball hard!
George had to run
very fast.

¡Crack!
¡Marco bateó muy fuerte la pelota!
Jorge tuvo que correr muy rápido.

George made it around the bases! It was Marco's first home run. George was happy to change the scoreboard. The Cubby Bears had won 5–4!

¡Jorge pasó por todas las bases! Era el primer jonrón de Marco. Jorge estaba contento de haber cambiado el marcador. ¡Los Oseznos ganaron 5 a 4!

Rules of the Game

Here are some basic baseball facts.

- **2** teams play against each other.
- There are always **9** players on the field:
    - A pitcher
    - A catcher
    - Players at first, second, and third base
    - Players in left field, right field, and centerfield
    - A shortstop
- There are **9 innings** in a baseball game.
- The winning team is the one that has scored the most runs at the end of nine innings.
- A team scores a run when a player crosses **home plate**.
- Each team has **3 outs** per inning.
- An out is made when
    - a batter gets three strikes (a strike means the batter swung the bat but missed the ball!);
    - a player in the field catches a hit ball before it touches the ground;
    - or a player does not get to the next base before the ball does.

There are other ways to make an out, but these are the most common!

- There are **3 bases** on a baseball field, plus home plate.
- If a batter hits the ball and makes it to first base, that is called a **single**.
- If a batter hits the ball and makes it to second base, that is a **double**.
- When the batter hits the ball and makes it to third base after a hit, that is a **triple**.
- You might already know what happens if a player hits the ball far enough away (usually right out of the park!) to make it to home plate—that's a **home run!**

PLAY BALL!

Reglas del juego

He aquí algunas normas básicas del béisbol.

- **2** equipos juegan uno contra el otro.
- Siempre hay **9** jugadores en el campo:
  - Un lanzador
  - Un receptor
  - Jugadores en la primera, segunda y tercera base
  - Jugadores en el campo izquierdo, campo derecho y campo central
  - Un torpedero
- Hay **9 entradas** en un partido de béisbol.
- Gana el equipo que tiene más carreras al final de las nueve entradas.
- Un equipo consigue una carrera cuando un jugador cruza **el plato**.
- Cada equipo tiene **3 *outs*** por entrada.
- Hay un *out* cuando
  - un bateador hace tres *strikes* (¡un *strike* significa que el bateador batea pero no golpea la pelota!);
  - un jugador del campo atrapa la pelota antes de que toque el suelo;
  - o cuando un jugador no llega a la siguiente base antes que la pelota.

¡Hay otras formas de hacer un *out,* pero estas son las más comunes!

- Hay **3 bases** en un campo de béisbol, además del plato.
- Si un bateador golpea la pelota y llega a la primera base, esto se llama **un sencillo**.
- Si un bateador golpea la pelota y llega a la segunda base, esto se llama **un doble**.
- Cuando el bateador golpea la pelota y llega a la tercera base, esto es **un triple**.
- Quizás ya sabes lo que pasa cuando un jugador golpea la pelota tan lejos (¡a menudo fuera del estadio!) que llega al plato—¡es un **jonrón**!

¡JUEGA AL BÉISBOL!